S. R.

The Balance Keepers

First edition

This book was professionally typeset on Reedsy.
Find out more at reedsy.com

Contents

One

Chapter 1

"I never asked for this. I never wanted to be the chosen one, the one destined to defeat the darkness that plagues our world. But fate has a funny way of choosing its champions, and it seems I am the only one left."

I sit alone in my room, staring at the faint glow of the candle on my nightstand. The shadows dance across the walls, taunting me with their whispers of fear and doubt. I can feel the weight of the world on my shoulders, the burden of a thousand lives resting upon my frail frame. I am not strong, not like the heroes of legend. I am just a timid girl, lost in a world of monsters and magic. And yet, somehow, it is up to me to save us all.

Two

Chapter 1: The Call

I never asked for this. I never wanted to be the chosen one, the one destined to defeat the darkness that plagues our world. But fate has a funny way of choosing its champions, and it seems I am the only one left.

My name is Alice, and I am just a normal girl. Or at least, I used to be. Now, I am something more, something greater. I am the hero, the savior, the one who has been called upon to defeat the evil that threatens to consume us all.

It started on a cold winter night, as I lay huddled under my blankets, trying to escape the icy chill that seeped through the cracks in the window. I was drifting off to sleep when I heard a voice, soft and distant, calling my name.

At first, I thought it was just my imagination, a product of my overactive mind. But the voice persisted, growing louder and clearer until it was impossible to ignore. It was a voice of desperation, of urgency, and it filled me with a sense of dread.

I sat up in bed, my heart racing, and listened as the voice spoke to me. It told me of the darkness that had awoken, of the ancient evil that threatened to engulf the world in shadow. And it told me that I was the only one who could stop it.

I wanted to run, to hide, to pretend that I had never heard the voice at all.

But I knew that I couldn't ignore it, not if I wanted to save the people I loved. So, with a heavy heart, I accepted my destiny and set out on a journey that would change my life forever.

As I left my home and stepped into the unknown, I knew that I was no longer just Alice, the timid girl. I was something more, something stronger. I was the hero, the one who would stand against the darkness and fight for the light.

There were 3 more chosen. First, there was Marcus, a gruff but kind-hearted warrior who had dedicated his life to fighting the darkness. He was the one who had answered the call of the voice, and he offered to join me on my quest, offering his sword and his strength to aid me.

Then, there was Elena, a clever and resourceful healer who had dedicated her life to helping others. She too had heard the call, and she offered to join us, offering her knowledge and her magic to heal our wounds and guide us on our way.

Finally, there was Jack, a mischievous and quick-witted thief who had a habit of finding himself in the wrong place at the right time. He had stumbled upon our group by chance, and though he had no desire to join our quest, he offered to help us in any way he could, using his skills and his cunning to get us out of sticky situations.

Together, the four of us set out on a journey that would take us across the land, facing dangers and challenges at every turn. But we were determined to succeed, driven by a sense of purpose and a bond that had formed between us.

And as we journeyed on, I began to see that I was not alone in my doubts and fears. Each of my companions had their own struggles, their own demons to face. But together, we were stronger than we could have ever been alone.

As we journeyed on, the bond between us grew stronger with each passing day. We faced countless dangers and challenges together, fighting side by side against the forces of darkness that threatened to consume us. And through it all, we supported each other, encouraging and inspiring one another to be our best selves.

Marcus proved to be a reliable and skilled warrior, always ready to throw himself into the fray to protect us. His gruff exterior belied a deep sense of loyalty and honor, and I came to see him as a mentor and a friend.

Elena was a constant source of healing and support, using her magic to mend our wounds and lift our spirits. She was kind and compassionate, always putting others before herself, and I came to see her as a sister and a confidante.

And Jack, despite his mischievous ways, proved to be a valuable ally, using his quick wit and clever tricks to get us out of countless tight spots. His sense of humor and irreverent attitude kept us all on our toes, and I came to see him as a brother and a partner in crime.

Together, the four of us faced every obstacle as a team, and I began to realize that we shared a common fate, a dark and dangerous destiny that had brought us together. We were no longer just strangers, united by circumstance. We were friends, bonded by a sense of purpose and a desire to make a difference in the world.

As we journeyed on, I began to see that I was not alone in my doubts and fears. Each of my companions had their own struggles, their own demons to face.

It was a cold and rainy night, and we had been traveling for days without a break. We were all exhausted and hungry, and as we huddled around the campfire, we knew that we needed a good meal to lift our spirits.

That's when Jack stepped up, pulling out a small bag of supplies from his pack. "Don't worry, kids," he said with a wink. "I've got this. Let's see what we can rustle up."

Despite his mischievous ways, Jack had a hidden talent for cooking, and he set to work with a flair that surprised us all. He pulled out a handful of herbs from his bag, tossing them into a pot of boiling water to create a savory broth. Then, he reached into his pack again, pulling out a small rabbit that he had caught earlier that day.

"Ah ha!" he exclaimed, holding up the rabbit triumphantly. "Dinner is served!"

He skinned and cleaned the rabbit with lightning speed, then cut it into small pieces and tossed it into the pot. As the rabbit cooked, the aroma wafted through the camp, making our stomachs growl with hunger.

But Jack wasn't done yet. With a flourish, he pulled out a small bag of dried fruits and nuts, and added them to the pot as well. "This will give it some extra flavor," he said with a grin.

Soon, the pot was bubbling with a rich, savory stew, and we all gathered around, eager to dig in. Jack ladled out generous portions for each of us, and we dug in with gusto, savoring the warmth and comfort of the meal.

As we ate, we talked and laughed, sharing stories of our journey so far. Marcus regaled us with tales of his battles against the darkness, while Elena told us of her adventures as a healer. And Jack, of course, had a story for every occasion, always ready with a quick joke or a witty remark.

It was a simple meal, but it was one of the best I had ever had. And as we sat around the campfire, full and content, I knew that we had become more than just a group of travelers. We were friends, united by a common goal and a shared sense of purpose.

We had been traveling for weeks, facing countless dangers and challenges as we made our way across the land. But despite our efforts, we knew that our journey was far from over. The voice that had called to me on that cold winter night had told us that our destiny lay at the foot of a distant mountain, a place of great darkness and danger.

And so, we pressed on, determined to reach our destination and face whatever lay ahead.

As we approached the mountain, a sense of foreboding filled the air. The sky was dark and stormy, and the ground shook with the rumble of thunder. It was as if the very earth was warning us to turn back, to flee from the danger that lay ahead.

But we had come too far to turn back now. We had to see this through to the end, no matter what the cost.

And then, as if in answer to our determination, a small bird appeared before us, its wings beating frantically as it struggled to stay aloft in the gusty winds. It was a messenger, sent to guide us on our way.

"Follow me!" it chirped, its voice clear and urgent. "A dark fate awaits you at the mountain. But there is still time to turn back, if you have the courage."

We looked at each other, our determination wavering. The bird's words filled us with fear and doubt, but we knew that we had to see this through to the end.

"We will follow you," I said, speaking for all of us. "Lead the way, and we will face whatever lies ahead together."

And so, with the bird leading the way, we set out towards the mountain, determined to see this journey through to the end. The fate that awaited us there was uncertain.

I couldn't help but think back to the life I had left behind. I thought of my family, my parents and my siblings, and the happy memories we had shared together.

I remembered the warmth of the sun on my face as we played in the fields, chasing butterflies and chasing each other. I remembered the laughter and the joy that filled our home, and the love that bound us together.

I remembered my mother's soft voice as she sang me to sleep at night, and the way my father's eyes would twinkle with pride when he looked at me. I remembered the simple pleasures of life, the small moments that had once seemed so insignificant, but now seemed so precious and dear.

And as I thought of all that I had left behind, a wave of sadness washed over me. I couldn't help but wonder if I would ever see my family again, or if I was doomed to wander the land alone, fighting a battle that seemed impossible to win.

But then I felt a hand on my shoulder, and I turned to see Marcus looking at me with concern. "Are you all right?" he asked, his voice soft and gentle.

I nodded, trying to push away the sadness that threatened to overwhelm me. "I'm fine," I said, forcing a smile. "I was just thinking about my family."

"I understand," Marcus said, his eyes filled with understanding. "It's hard to leave behind the ones we love. But we have a duty to fulfill, a purpose that is greater than ourselves. And we must be strong, for their sake, as well as our own."

I nodded, knowing that he was right. My family was counting on me, and I couldn't let them down. I had to be strong, and I had to see this through to the end.

And so, with a renewed sense of determination, I turned my face towards the mountain, ready to face whatever lay ahead. The fate that awaited us there was uncertain, but I knew that I was not alone.

Three

Chapter 2: The Ascent

We reached the mountain at dawn, the morning sun casting a golden glow over the rugged peaks. The journey had been long and arduous, but we were finally here, ready to face whatever lay ahead.

As we gazed up at the towering mountain, a sense of awe and reverence filled me. I had never seen anything like it, and I couldn't help but wonder what secrets lay hidden within its depths.

But as we prepared to make our ascent, I couldn't shake off the feeling of dread that weighed upon me. I knew that this was the moment we had been preparing for, the moment when our destiny would be revealed. And I couldn't help but wonder if we were truly ready for what lay ahead.

As we set off towards the mountain, Marcus stayed by my side, his presence a constant comfort. He was a skilled and formidable warrior, and I knew that he would do everything in his power to protect me.

But as we journeyed on, I began to see that there was more to Marcus than just his strength and his skills. He was kind and compassionate, always putting others before himself. And as we spent more time together, I found myself drawn to him, drawn to the warmth and kindness that radiated from him.

It was a small thing, a fleeting moment of connection, but it was enough. And as we journeyed on, I knew that I had found a friend, and perhaps something more, in Marcus.

We reached the base of the mountain just as the sun was setting, and we made camp for the night. As we sat around the campfire, sharing stories and laughter

We set off early the next morning, our determination renewed. The mountain loomed before us, a daunting challenge that we were determined to overcome.

As we made our way up the steep, rocky path, Marcus stayed by my side, always ready to lend a hand or offer a word of encouragement. He was a skilled and formidable warrior, and I knew that he would do everything in his power to protect me.

And as we journeyed on, I began to see that there was more to Marcus than just his strength and his skills. He was kind and compassionate, always putting others before himself. And as we spent more time together, I found myself drawn to him, drawn to the warmth and kindness that radiated from him.

It was a small thing, a fleeting moment of connection, but it was enough. And as we journeyed on, I knew that I had found a friend, and perhaps something more, in Marcus.

As we reached the halfway point of our ascent, Marcus stopped and turned to me. "I want you to have this," he said, holding out his sword.

I looked at the weapon in surprise. It was a finely crafted sword, with a blade that was worn and scratched from countless battles. It was a weapon of great power and strength, and I knew that it was a symbol of Marcus's skills and his dedication to his craft.

"I can't take your sword," I protested. "It's your most prized possession."

"It's not just a weapon," Marcus said, his eyes serious. "It's a symbol of my commitment to the cause. And I want you to have it, as a sign of my support and my loyalty. I know that you are the hero of this journey, and I want you to have the best weapon I can give you."

I looked at the sword, overwhelmed by Marcus's gesture. It was a symbol of his trust and his faith in me, and I knew that I could not refuse it.

"Thank you," I said, my voice filled with emotion. "I will treasure it always."

We reached the top of the mountain at midday, the sun beating down upon us with a fierce intensity. We were exhausted and thirsty, but we were determined to see this through to the end.

As we approached the summit, we saw a figure waiting for us, silhouetted against the bright sky. It was a man, tall and gaunt, with a cloak of darkness swirling around him.

"Who are you?" I called out, my voice echoing through the still air.

"I am the abyss mage," the man replied, his voice a hiss of hatred. "I am the one who summoned you here, to face your destiny and your doom."

I looked at Marcus and Elena, knowing that this was the moment we had been preparing for. The abyss mage was the one who had awoken the darkness, the one who threatened to engulf the world in shadow. And we were the ones who had been called upon to stop him.

We drew our weapons, ready to face the mage in battle. But as we approached, we saw that he was not alone. A horde of shadowy figures surrounded him, their eyes glowing with an otherworldly light.

The battle was fierce and brutal, with the mage unleashing wave after wave of dark magic against us. But we were determined to fight, fueled by our sense of purpose and our bond of friendship.

"We won't let you win!" I shouted, swinging my sword with all my might.

"You don't stand a chance against us!" Marcus yelled, his sword flashing as he fought off the shadowy figures.

"We will stop you, no matter what it takes!" Elena cried, unleashing a burst of healing magic to aid us in battle.

Suddenly, the ground shook with a mighty rumble, and from the shadows emerged a horde of undead animals, their eyes glowing with a sinister light. There were wolves and bears, their fur matted and their teeth bared, and snakes and spiders, their venomous fangs glistening in the sun.

We fought with all our strength, but the undead creatures were relentless, driven by the mage's dark magic. They swarmed around us, their claws and fangs tearing at our flesh.

"We have to stop him!" I shouted, swinging my sword with all my might. "We can't let him unleash this darkness on the world!"

"We won't give up!" Marcus yelled, his sword flashing as he fought off the undead beasts. "We will defeat him, no matter what it takes!"

"We will stop him, together!" Elena cried, unleashing a burst of healing magic to aid us in battle.

The mage laughed, his voice filled with contempt. "You are nothing but insects, crawling at my feet. You will all fall before me, and the darkness will engulf the world!"

But we would not be defeated. We fought with all our strength

The battle raged on, with both sides determined to emerge victorious. But as the hours passed, it became clear that this would be a fight to the death.

The mage was a formidable opponent, unleashing wave after wave of dark magic against us. But we were determined to stop him, fueled by our sense of purpose and our bond of friendship.

As the battle reached its climax, Marcus stepped forward, his sword drawn and his eyes burning with determination. "I will not let you win," he shouted, his voice echoing through the air. "I will stop you, no matter what it takes!"

With a mighty cry, Marcus launched himself at the mage, his sword flashing with a fierce light. The mage raised his staff, unleashing a blast of dark magic that knocked Marcus to the ground.

"You are no match for me," the mage sneered, his voice filled with contempt. "You are nothing but a fool, throwing your life away in a vain attempt to defeat me."

But Marcus was not defeated. With a fierce determination, he struggled to his feet, his sword still clenched in his hand. "I will not let you win," he said, his voice filled with a fierce resolve. "I will stop you, no matter what it takes."

And with that, Marcus charged at the mage, his sword raised high. The mage raised his staff, ready to unleash another blast of dark magic, but it was too late. Marcus's sword struck home, piercing the mage's heart and ending his reign of darkness forever.

As the mage fell to the ground, a great cry of triumph rose up from our ranks.

The battle was over, and we had emerged victorious. The mage lay at our feet, his reign of darkness ended forever.

We stood there, panting and sweat-drenched, but filled with a sense of triumph and joy. We had done it - we had saved the world from the darkness that threatened to engulf it.

As we basked in the glow of our victory, a small bird appeared before us, its wings beating frantically as it struggled to stay aloft in the gusty winds. It was the same bird that had led us to the mountain, the messenger that had guided us on our journey.

"Next your adventure awaits at the city of gold."

Four

Chapter 3: Lust

As we journeyed on, we were filled with excitement and wonder at the thought of reaching this legendary city. We had heard so much about it, and we couldn't wait to see it with our own eyes.

At last, after many days of travel, we reached the City of Gold. As we approached its gates, we were awed by its beauty and splendor. The city was a place of wonder, with towering spires of gold and crystal, and streets paved with shimmering jewels.

We made our way through the city, marveling at the sights and sounds that surrounded us. Everywhere we looked, there were people, dressed in the finest garments and jewels, living in opulence and luxury.

As we walked through the streets, we were greeted with cheers and applause, for we were hailed as heroes, the ones who had saved the world from the darkness that threatened to engulf it.

We spent many days in the City of Gold, reveling in its beauty and splendor. We visited its temples and palaces, its markets and gardens, and we were awed by the wonders that we saw.

Five

Chapter 3: The City of Gold (continued)

One of the first places we visited in the City of Gold was the golden casino, a place of wonder and enchantment. We had heard tales of its opulence and splendor, and we couldn't wait to see it for ourselves.

As we walked through the doors of the golden casino, we were awed by the sights and sounds that greeted us. Everywhere we looked, there were people, dressed in the finest garments and jewels, gambling and reveling in the glow of the golden light.

We made our way through the casino, our senses heightened by the sights and sounds around us. There were games of chance and skill, with people from all walks of life gathered around the tables, vying for their chance at fortune and glory.

I was drawn to the roulette table, mesmerized by the spinning wheel and the silver ball that danced across the numbers. I placed my bet and held my breath, hoping for the lucky spin that would bring me riches beyond my wildest dreams.

But luck was not on my side that day, and I walked away from the roulette table empty-handed. Still, I was filled with excitement and wonder at the magic of the golden casino, and I knew that I would be back, ready to try my luck once again.

We spent many hours in the golden casino, marveling at the wonders that surrounded us. And as we left, our pockets empty but our hearts full.

But as the night wore on, the feeling of danger only grew stronger. We heard whispers and murmurs, secrets spoken in hushed tones. And as we walked past a shadowy corner, we saw a flash of steel, the glint of a blade.

We froze, our hearts racing with fear. We knew, in that moment, that we were in grave danger. The golden casino was a trap, a setup for an assassination.

We drew our weapons, ready to defend ourselves. But it was too late. A group of assassins emerged from the shadows, their blades drawn and their eyes cold and lifeless.

We fought with all our might, but we were outnumbered and outmatched. And as the blades closed in around us, we knew that our journey might come to an end.

But even as we faced our doom, we knew that we had lived a life filled with adventure and purpose. We had faced countless dangers and challenges before.

Marcus immediately stepped forward, his hand on the hilt of his sword. "Who are you and what do you want?" he demanded.

One of the Assassins sneered at him. "We've been hired to eliminate you and your companions," he said, drawing a pair of daggers from his belt.

Elena stepped up beside Marcus, her fists clenched at her sides. "We're not going down without a fight," she said determinedly.

Jack, meanwhile, had already taken out a small crossbow and was loading it with a bolt. "I'll take out as many of these guys as I can," he said, his eyes narrowed in determination.

As the Assassins advanced on us, I reached for the short sword at my belt. I might not have had powers like them, but I was a skilled fighter and I was ready to take them on.

The fight was intense and brutal.

One of the Assassins landed a powerful blow, sending Jack flying across the room. He hit the ground with a thud and lay there motionless.

I rushed over to him, my heart pounding in my chest. "Jack, are you okay?" I shouted, trying to shake him awake. But he didn't respond.

I turned to Marcus and Elena, tears streaming down my face. "We have to do something, he's not breathing!"

But it was too late. Jack had taken a fatal blow and there was nothing we could do to save him, not even heal him.

As we stood there, grief-stricken and heartbroken, I couldn't help but think about all the adventures we had shared together. Jack had been a loyal friend and a brave companion, and I would never forget him.

It hit me like a punch to the gut, and I knew that things would never be the same without him. The Golden Casino had claimed another victim, and we were left to mourn the loss of our dear friend.

Still reeling from the loss of Jack, a brilliant flash of light caught our attention. I turned to see the great phoenix bird descending from the sky, its wings spread wide and its feathers shimmering in the light.

The bird landed gracefully in front of us, its eyes seeming to pierce right through us. "Congratulations on your victory," it said, its voice carrying a sense of pride and respect. "You have proven yourselves to be skilled and brave warriors."

I couldn't believe what I was hearing. Was this real, or was it some kind of hallucination brought on by the stress of the battle?

But the pheonix seemed very real, and it continued to speak. "Your journey is not over yet," it said. "You must go to the ancient ruins of the Lost City, where you will find the answers you seek."

I looked at Marcus and Elena, who both seemed just as stunned as I was. "The Lost City?" I repeated, trying to wrap my head around this new information.

The pheonix nodded. "There, you will find the answers you have been seeking, and perhaps even a way to bring Jack back."

With that, the bird spread its wings and took flight, disappearing into the sky.

I looked at Marcus and Elena, my heart heavy with grief but also filled with hope. "We have to go to the Lost City," I said determinedly. "We have to find a way to bring Jack back."

Together, we set out on our journey to the Lost City, determined to uncover its secrets and bring our friend back to life.

Six

Chapter 5: The Lost City

As we approached the ancient ruins of the Lost City, I couldn't help but feel a sense of awe and wonder. The crumbling stone structures seemed to stretch on for miles, surrounded by a dense jungle that seemed to almost pulse with life.

We followed the winding path through the jungle, taking care to avoid the vines and thorns that seemed to reach out to snag us as we passed. The air was thick and humid, and I could feel beads of sweat rolling down my face as we trudged on.

Finally, we emerged into a clearing, where we were confronted with the most breathtaking sight I had ever seen. In the center of the clearing stood a massive pyramid, its stone walls adorned with intricate carvings and symbols.

As we approached, I couldn't help but feel a sense of foreboding. Something about this place seemed off, like there was some kind of ancient power lurking just beneath the surface.

Despite my reservations, we pressed on, determined to find the answers we had come seeking. We made our way up the pyramid, our footsteps echoing off the stone as we climbed.

At the top, we were confronted with a massive stone door, inscribed with more of the strange symbols we had seen throughout the ruins.

With a deep breath, I pushed the door open, revealing a dark and foreboding chamber within. But we didn't let that deter us.

As we made our way through the chamber, I couldn't shake the feeling that we were being watched. The air was thick with the scent of incense and the sound of chanting seemed to fill the air.

We followed the sound of the chanting to a room filled with strange altars and ancient artifacts. In the center of the room stood a group of hooded figures, their faces obscured in shadow.

One of them stepped forward, holding out a hand to us. "Welcome, travelers," the figure said in a deep, guttural voice. "You have come seeking the power of the Lost City, but be warned. Such power comes with a price."

I looked at Marcus and Elena, my heart racing. What did these people want from us, and were we prepared to pay the price for their power?

As we stood there, trying to decide what to do, a bright light suddenly filled the room. We turned to see a glowing orb floating in the air, its radiance almost blinding.

The orb spoke to us, its voice filled with wisdom and understanding. "Do not be afraid," it said. "I am the guardian of the Lost City, and I have been watching over you on your journey. You have proven yourselves to be worthy of the power that lies within these ruins."

I looked at Marcus and Elena, my heart filled with hope and excitement. Could this be the answer we had been seeking, a way to bring Jack back to life?

As we stood in the chamber, gazing at the glowing orb, a group of ancient South American gods appeared before us. They were majestic and powerful, their forms shimmering and ethereal.

"Greetings, travelers," one of them said, his voice echoing through the chamber. "We have been watching your journey, and we have seen the loss you have suffered. We offer you the chance to bring your comrade back to life, if you are willing to pay the price."

I looked at Marcus and Elena, my heart racing with excitement and hope. Could this be the answer we had been seeking?

But as I looked at the gods, I couldn't shake the feeling that something was off. What did they want in return for their power, and were we prepared to pay the price?

Despite my reservations, I stepped forward, ready to do whatever it took to bring Jack back. "We accept your offer," I said firmly.

The gods nodded, their eyes glowing with a strange, otherworldly light. "Very well," one of them said. "But be warned, the price is steep. Are you prepared to make the ultimate sacrifice?"

I took a deep breath, steeling myself for whatever lay ahead. "Yes," I said. "We will do whatever it takes."

With that, the gods began the ritual, their chanting filling the air as they called forth the power of the Lost City. As the light grew brighter and brighter, I closed my eyes.

"In order to bring your comrade back to life, you must all give up a part of your life force," one of the gods said, his voice echoing through the chamber. "Only by sacrificing a part of yourselves can you hope to bring your friend back."

I looked at Marcus and Elena, my heart heavy with grief and uncertainty. Could we really make such a sacrifice, knowing that it would shorten our own lives?

But as I thought about Jack, and all the adventures we had shared together, I knew that I couldn't just stand by and do nothing. I would do whatever it took to bring him back.

With a sense of determination, I stepped forward. "We accept," I said firmly. "We will make the sacrifice."

The gods nodded, their eyes glowing with approval. And as the ritual began, I closed my eyes, praying that our sacrifice would be worth it.

As the life force flowed from our bodies, I couldn't help but feel a sense of peace and acceptance. If this was what it took to bring Jack back, then it was a price I was willing to pay.

Finally, the ritual was complete, and the gods stepped back, their work done.

Marcus: "I can't believe it, Jack is back! I thought we'd lost you forever."

Elena: "I was so worried about you. It's a miracle that you're alive."

Alice: "I'm just so grateful that we're all together again. I don't know what I would have done without you guys."

Jack: "I can't even begin to thank you all for bringing me back. I don't know how it happened, but I'm just so grateful to be alive."

Marcus: "We couldn't have done it without Alice. She's the one who figured out how to bring you back."

Elena: "Yeah, she's a real genius. And she never gave up, even when everyone else thought it was impossible."

Alice: "I just couldn't accept that we'd lost you. I had to do everything I could to bring you back."

Jack: "Well, you succeeded. And I'll never be able to repay you for that. You're all the best friends a guy could ask for."

Elena: "We're just glad to have you back, Jack. We were all so worried about you."

Seven

Chapter 6: Roots

As the sun began to set over the small village nestled in the heart of the forest, Elena sat by the fireplace in her childhood home, lost in thought. She remembered the long, hot summers spent running barefoot through the fields, the cool autumn nights huddled around the bonfire with her friends, and the freezing winters spent huddled under blankets, listening to her mother's stories of magic and adventure.

But as much as she loved her childhood, there was one memory that always stuck with her, a memory of fear and pain. It was the memory of the day she discovered her roots, the day she learned the truth about who she really was.

She had always known that she was different from the other children in the village, with her bright green eyes and wild, untamed hair. But it wasn't until that fateful day that she learned the true extent of her difference. She had always been told that her mother was a simple forest-dweller, but as it turned out, her mother was so much more.

Elena's mother was a powerful sorceress, descended from a long line of magic users. And as Elena's powers began to manifest, it became clear that she was destined to follow in her mother's footsteps.

But the path of a magic user was fraught with danger, and as Elena delved deeper into the world of the supernatural, she realized that she was not alone.

There were others out there like her, people with gifts and abilities beyond the ordinary, and they were not always kind.

As the flames in the fireplace flickered and danced, Elena had no idea that she had a long, difficult journey ahead of her.

Elena's heritage was a mix of Latin and forest-dweller, a combination that was rare and often misunderstood by those around her. She was proud of her Latin roots, with their rich history and vibrant culture, but she also knew that being different could be challenging at times.

Growing up, Elena often felt torn between two worlds. She loved the traditions and values of her Latin ancestors, but she also loved the freedom and wildness of the forest, where her mother had raised her. She often found herself caught between the expectations of her community and her own desire to forge her own path.

Despite the difficulties, Elena embraced her heritage with pride. She learned to speak fluent Spanish and studied the ancient mythology and folklore of her ancestors. She also learned to dance the salsa and other traditional Latin dances, and she loved nothing more than to lose herself in the music and the movement.

As she grew older and her magical powers became more pronounced, Elena began to understand the true meaning of her heritage. She came to realize that her Latin ancestry and her forest-dweller roots were not mutually exclusive, but rather two parts of a whole.

As the plane touched down in Tokyo, Elena couldn't contain her excitement. She had always dreamed of visiting Japan, with its bustling cities and ancient temples, and now that dream was finally becoming a reality.

She, Jack, Marcus, and Alice were a team of adventurers, traveling the world in search of new experiences and challenges. They had been planning this trip to Tokyo for months, and now that they were finally here, Elena could hardly believe it.

As they stepped off the plane and into the bustling airport, they were immediately struck by the sights and sounds of the city. Everywhere they looked, there were people rushing past, the air filled with the sounds of chatter and the smells of food.

Elena couldn't wait to explore everything that Tokyo had to offer. They had planned to stay for a week, and she was determined to make the most of it. They had a list of must-see attractions and activities, and she was eager to check them all off.

First on the list was a visit to the famous Shibuya Crossing, where hundreds of people crossed the street at once in a chaotic blur of bodies and lights. Elena's heart raced as they joined the throngs of people, jostling their way through the crowd and trying to keep up with Marcus, who seemed to know exactly where he was going.

As they emerged on the other side, Elena couldn't help but laugh with excitement. This was just the beginning of their adventure in Tokyo, and she couldn't wait to see what else the city had in store for them.

As they stood at the edge of the crowded intersection, Marcus turned to the others and spoke in a serious tone. "Remember, everyone, we need to be careful while we're here. The bird sent us to Tokyo for a reason, and we don't know what we might be up against."

Elena nodded, her excitement dimming slightly at Marcus's words. She knew that their adventures often led them into dangerous situations, and she trusted Marcus's instincts. He had a way of sensing when something was off, and she knew better than to ignore his warnings.

"What do you think we're up against?" asked Alice, her eyes scanning the crowd nervously.

"I'm not sure," Marcus replied. "But we need to be prepared for anything. Stay alert, and stick together."

Elena and the others nodded, their expressions serious. They knew that they had to be ready for anything, and they were determined to see this mission through to the end, no matter what obstacles they might face.

As they set off into the crowded streets of Tokyo, Elena couldn't shake the feeling that they were being watched. She kept her senses heightened, alert for any sign of danger. She knew that Marcus was right - they needed to be careful if they wanted to make it out of Tokyo alive.

As they made their way towards Shibuya Crossing, Elena couldn't shake the feeling that someone was following them. She kept turning around, trying to catch a glimpse of their pursuer, but the crowds were too thick and she couldn't see anything.

"Do you guys feel like we're being followed?" she asked, glancing at Jack and Alice.

"I've been feeling it too," Jack replied, his brow furrowed. "I can't see anyone, but I can definitely sense someone back there."

"Me too," Alice added, her eyes darting around the crowd. "I don't know if it's a friendly monk or something more sinister."

"We need to be careful," Marcus said, his voice low. "Keep your eyes and ears open, and stay close to me. If anything happens, we need to be ready to defend ourselves."

Elena nodded, her heart racing. She couldn't shake the feeling that they were in danger, and she knew that they needed to be ready for anything. As they approached Shibuya Crossing, she kept her senses heightened, ready to act if necessary.

But as they reached the crowded intersection and the crowds swirled around them, their pursuer seemed to vanish. Elena couldn't see anyone following them, and she couldn't sense anyone nearby. She let out a sigh of relief, but she knew that they needed to stay alert. They were in a strange place, and they couldn't afford to let their guard down.

As they stood at the edge of the crowded intersection, trying to decide which way to go, they suddenly felt a tap on their shoulder. Elena turned to see a friendly-looking monk standing behind them, a warm smile on his face.

"Hello, friends," the monk said in perfect English. "It seems you are a little lost. May I be of assistance?"

Elena and the others looked at each other in surprise. They had been so focused on the feeling of being followed that they hadn't even noticed the monk approaching them.

"Yes, thank you," Marcus said, recovering his composure. "We're trying to find our way to the temple."

"Ah, the temple," the monk nodded. "I can show you the way. It is not far from here. Follow me."

Elena and the others followed the monk through the crowded streets, relieved to finally have some guidance. As they walked, the monk told them about the history and traditions of the temple, and Elena found herself feeling more at ease.

As they approached the temple gates, the monk turned to them and bowed. "I must leave you now, but I hope you will visit the temple and find peace and enlightenment within its walls."

Elena thanked the monk and watched as he walked away, his robes rustling in the breeze. She couldn't help but feel grateful for the chance encounter, and she knew that they had the monk to thank for their safe arrival at the temple.

As they stood at the gates of the temple, watching the friendly monk walk away, Elena couldn't shake the feeling that they would see him again. She didn't know how she knew, but something about the monk seemed familiar, almost as if they had met before.

"Do you guys get the feeling that we've met that monk before?" she asked, turning to Jack and Alice.

"I do," Alice nodded. "I can't explain it, but I feel like I know him."

"Me too," Jack agreed. "Maybe we met him on one of our previous adventures."

"Could be," Marcus said, thoughtfully. "But we should focus on the task at hand. We have a lot to do while we're here in Tokyo, and we can't afford to get sidetracked."

Elena nodded, pushing aside her thoughts of the monk. Marcus was right - they had a job to do, and they needed to stay focused. But as they entered the temple and began to explore its ancient halls, she couldn't help but wonder if they would see the friendly monk again.

As they explored the temple, Elena couldn't shake the feeling that they were being watched. She kept turning around, trying to catch a glimpse of their pursuer, but the crowds were too thick and she couldn't see anyone.

"Do you guys feel like we're being followed?" she asked, glancing at Jack and Alice.

"I've been feeling it too," Jack replied, his brow furrowed. "I can't see anyone, but I can definitely sense someone back there."

"Me too," Alice added, her eyes darting around the crowd. "I don't know if it's a friendly monk or something more sinister."

"We need to be careful," Marcus said, his voice low. "Keep your eyes and ears open, and stay close to me. If anything happens, we need to be ready to defend ourselves."

Elena nodded, her heart racing. She couldn't shake the feeling that they were in danger, and she knew that they needed to be ready for anything. As they moved through the temple, she kept her senses heightened, ready to act if necessary.

But despite their vigilance, they couldn't find any sign of their pursuer. It was as if they had vanished into thin air. Elena couldn't help but feel relieved, but she knew that they needed to stay alert. They were in a strange place, and they couldn't afford to let their guard down.

Just as she was about to call out to the others, she heard a sudden cry of alarm. She turned to see that Alice had fallen into a pit, her arms flailing as she tried to grab onto the sides.

"Alice!" Elena shouted, running towards her. "Hold on, I'll get you out of there!"

She reached the pit and saw that Alice was struggling to climb out, but the sides were too steep and she kept slipping back down. Elena knew that she had to do something fast - they couldn't leave Alice down there.

"Hold on, I'm coming!" she called, searching for a way to reach her.

She grabbed onto a nearby vine and swung herself down into the pit, landing next to Alice. She saw that Alice had been bitten by a venomous snake, and she knew that they had to get her out of there before it was too late.

"Hold on, Alice," she said, trying to keep her voice steady. "We're going to get you out of here."

She grabbed onto Alice and helped her to her feet, and together they climbed out of the pit. As they emerged into the sunlight, Elena couldn't help but feel relieved. They had made it out alive, but she knew that they had to get Alice to safety as soon as possible.

"We have to get you to a hospital," she said, helping Alice to her feet. "You've been poisoned, and we have to get you help."

Alice nodded, her face pale and sweaty. Elena knew that they had to move fast if they wanted to save her. She helped Alice to her feet.

"Look here, it's an underground tunnel, Marcus exclaimed from the depths.

Elena and the others worked together, searching the underground chamber for a way out. They followed the faint glow of the torches, hoping to find an exit, but the tunnels seemed to go on forever.

Just when they were starting to lose hope, they finally saw a glimmer of light ahead. They followed it, their spirits lifting, and soon they emerged into the daylight.

Elena let out a sigh of relief as she emerged from the underground chamber, the bright sunshine blinding after the darkness of the tunnels. She turned to see Marcus, Jack, and Alice emerging behind her, looking just as relieved.

"We made it," Marcus said, a smile spreading across his face. "That was too close for comfort."

"No kidding," Elena agreed, grinning. "I don't think I want to go underground again anytime soon."

They took a moment to catch their breath, grateful to be out of danger. But they knew that they couldn't stay there for long - they had a mission to complete, and they couldn't afford to let their guard down.

As Elena and the others made their way through the dark, twisting tunnels of the underground cavern, they couldn't help but be awestruck by the beauty that surrounded them. The walls glowed with a faint, otherworldly light, and the air was filled with the sound of rushing water.

They had never seen anything like it - the cavern was like nothing they had ever encountered before. The walls were adorned with strange, intricate patterns, and the floors were smooth and polished, as if they had been carved by some ancient hand.

Everywhere they looked, they saw something new and fascinating. There were stalagmites rising up from the floor like giant teeth, and stalactites hanging from the ceiling like delicate icicles. The air was cool and damp, and the sound of dripping water echoed through the cavern.

As they made their way deeper into the cavern, they came across a series of strange, glowing mushrooms, their tops pulsing with a faint, blue light. Elena couldn't help but reach out and touch one, and was surprised to find that it was soft and spongy to the touch.

"What is this place?" Jack whispered, his voice filled with wonder. "It's like nothing I've ever seen before."

"I have no idea," Marcus replied, his eyes scanning the cavern. "But whatever it is, it's clear that we're not the first ones to discover it. Someone, or something, has been living here.

Just as Elena and the others were marveling at the beauty of the underground cavern, they heard a sudden, fierce roar echoing through the tunnels. They froze, their hearts racing, as the sound grew louder and closer.

"What was that?" Alice whispered, her eyes wide with fear.

"I don't know," Marcus said, his voice tense. "But whatever it is, it doesn't sound friendly."

Elena's pulse raced as she scanned the cavern, trying to see where the roar was coming from. She couldn't see anything, but she could feel the ground shaking beneath her feet.

"We have to get out of here," she said, her voice urgent. "Whatever it is, it's coming closer."

They turned and ran, their footsteps echoing through the tunnels as they tried to escape the approaching danger. Elena's heart pounded in her chest as she ran, her eyes fixed on the exit. She knew that they had to get out of there, and fast.

As they reached the entrance to the cavern, they burst out into the sunlight, panting and gasping for air. They collapsed on the ground, their hearts racing as they tried to catch their breath.

"What was that thing?" Alice asked, her voice shaking.

"I don't know," Marcus replied, his eyes scanning the cavern all over. "But whatever it was, I don't want to meet it again."

Elena nodded, her mind racing. Whatever that creature had been, it was clear that they had narrowly escaped with their lives. And as they gathered their things and set off once again, she couldn't shake the feeling that they were being watched.

Eight

Chapter 7: The World Dragon

Just when they were starting to think that they were imagining things, they heard a sudden roar echoing through the jungle. They froze, their hearts racing, as the sound grew louder and closer.

"What was that?" Alice whispered, her eyes wide with fear.

"I don't know," Marcus replied, his voice tense. "But whatever it is, it doesn't sound friendly."

Elena's pulse raced as she scanned the jungle, trying to see where the roar was coming from. And then, through the dense foliage, she saw a glimpse of a massive, scaly body.

"It's the world dragon!" she gasped, her eyes widening. "It's real!"

The others turned to see the legendary beast, its scales glinting in the sunlight. It let out another roar, its eyes blazing with a fierce intelligence.

"What do we do?" Alice asked, her voice trembling.

"I don't know," Marcus said, his eyes fixed on the dragon. "But we have to be careful. We don't want to anger it."

They knew that they were in the presence of a true legend, and she couldn't believe that they were actually seeing it with their own eyes. But as the dragon let out another roar, she knew that they had to be careful. They were in the presence of a powerful, ancient being, and they had to respect its power and might.

in awe of the legendary world dragon, they watched in amazement as it began to shimmer and transform before their eyes. The scales melted away, and the beast's body seemed to shrink and contort until it had taken on the shape of an old man.

The old man smiled at them, his eyes twinkling with amusement. "Well done, my friends," he said, his voice deep and resonant. "You have come far on your journey, and you have proven yourselves worthy of this final test."

Elena and the others looked at each other in surprise. They had never seen anything like it - the transformation from dragon to man had been so seamless and effortless.

"Who are you?" Marcus asked, his voice filled with awe.

"I am the world dragon," the old man replied. "I have been watching you from afar, and I have been impressed by your determination and bravery. You have proven yourselves to be worthy of this final challenge."

"What challenge?" Elena asked, her heart racing.

"Your last test lies in another world," the old man replied. "A world unlike any you have ever seen. You must journey there and defeat the demon king. Only once you do that will I reward you for your troubles"

Elena and the others looked at each other, their eyes filled with fear.

The legend of the world dragon and the demon king was one of the oldest and most revered in all the lands. It was said that in the beginning, the world was ruled by the demon king, a being of immense power and darkness. He ruled with an iron fist, and all who opposed him were crushed beneath his might.

But there was one being who resisted the demon king's rule - the world dragon. The world dragon was an ancient and powerful creature, a being of great wisdom and strength. It was said that the world dragon had lived for eons, watching over the world and protecting it from harm.

The demon king, however, was determined to bend the world dragon to his will. He summoned all his power and waged war against the dragon, hoping to enslave it and use its strength to conquer the world.

But the world dragon was not one to be easily defeated. It fought back with all its might, its flames and claws tearing through the demon king's army. The battle raged on for days, the earth shaking with the force of their clashes.

In the end, it was the world dragon who emerged victorious. It defeated the demon king and cast him into the depths of the earth, where he was sealed away for all eternity. The world dragon, however, chose to remain on the surface, watching over the world and protecting it from harm.

And so it was that the world dragon became the guardian of the world, revered by all mortals while the demon king possessed the support of every demon in chaos.

Nine

Chapter 8: The Final Battle

Alice and the others stood at the edge of the demon king's realm, their hearts racing as they prepared for the final battle. They had journeyed far and faced many challenges on their quest, but they knew that this would be the most difficult test of all.

The demon king's realm was a dark and twisted place, filled with danger at every turn. The air was thick with the stench of sulfur, and the ground was scorched and blackened by the fires of the underworld.

But Alice and the others were determined to see their mission through to the end. They had come too far to turn back now, and they knew that they had to face the demon king and put an end to his reign of terror.

They made their way through the twisted landscape, their senses heightened as they searched for the demon king's lair. They knew that he was somewhere nearby, and they had to be ready for anything.

As they approached the demon king's lair, they heard a faint rumbling noise. It grew louder and louder, until it became a deafening roar that shook the very ground beneath their feet.

Alice and the others turned to see the demon king emerging from his lair, his eyes blazing with hatred and malice. He was a massive, hulking creature, with skin as hard as steel and teeth like razor-sharp knives.

"So, you have come to challenge me," the demon king growled, his voice like thunder. "You are fools to think that you can defeat me. I am the ruler of this realm, and I will not be denied."

Alice and the others stood their ground, their hearts racing. They knew that they had to face the demon king, no matter how daunting the challenge.

"We've come to put an end to your reign of terror," Alice said, her voice fierce. "We won't let you rule over the world any longer."

The demon king let out a roar of anger and attacked. Alice and the others fought back with all their might, their swords flashing in the dim light. The battle raged on for what seemed like an eternity, the demon king's minions joining the fight.

Elana tried to use her healing powers to defend against the attack, but it was of no use. The minions were too numerous, and they were overwhelming her and the others.

It was looking like the end for Elana and the others, as they were surrounded on all sides by the demon king's minions. They fought with all their might, their swords flashing through the air, but they knew that they were outnumbered and outmatched.

Just when all hope seemed lost, a sudden bolt of lightning shot through the sky, striking the minions and sending them fleeing in all directions.

Elana and the others turned to see the world dragon standing behind them, its eyes blazing with power. It let out a fierce roar, its wings spread wide, and the minions scattered in fear.

The world dragon nodded, its eyes fixed on the demon king's lifeless body. "It is my duty to protect the world from evil," it said, its voice deep and resonant. "My body cannot handle being in this realm for long. Help me defeat evil companions."

The ground shook with the force of their clashes, and the air was thick with the smell of smoke and burning flesh.

Elana and the others turned to see the world dragon standing behind them, its eyes blazing with power. It let out a fierce roar, its wings spread wide, and the minions scattered in fear.

Together, they stood against the demon king, their swords flashing through the air. The battle raged on, the demon king unleashing all his power in a final, desperate attack.

the demon king let out a roar of anger and desperation. He knew that this was his final chance to defeat his enemies and continue his reign of terror.

He summoned all his power, his eyes blazing with malevolent energy. The ground shook with the force of his aura, and the air was thick with the smell of sulfur and death.

The world dragon and the others braced themselves for the worst, their swords flashing through the air as they prepared to face the demon king's ultimate attack.

The demon king unleashed a massive blast of energy, his power consuming everything in its path. The ground shook with the force of the attack, and Elana and the others were thrown back by the explosion.

But they refused to give up. Gathering their strength, they rose to their feet and stood against the demon king, their hearts filled with determination and courage.

Together, they fought back against the demon king's ultimate attack, their swords flashing through the air as they battled against the forces of darkness. The ground shook with the force of their clashes, and the air was filled with the sound of metal clashing against metal.

And in the end, good triumphed over evil as they stood in the battlefield exhausted beyond belief.

They had saved the world from the forces of darkness, and they knew that they had made a difference.

"We did it," Elana said, panting and sweating. "We defeated the demon king and saved the world."

The others nodded, their faces breaking into broad smiles. "We couldn't have done it without you," Marcus said, clapping Elana on the back.

"Or without each other," Alice added, her eyes shining with pride. "We make a pretty good team."

"We do," Jack agreed, his face breaking into a grin. "And we're not done yet. There will always be more challenges to face, but we'll face them together."

The world dragon nodded, its eyes fixed on the horizon. "The world is safe, for now," it said. "But there will always be more dangers to face. It is up to you and the others to protect it and keep the balance of good and evil in check."

Elana and the others nodded, their hearts filled with determination. They knew that their journey was far from over, and they were ready to face whatever challenges lay ahead. Together, they would protect the world and keep it safe for all eternity.

www.ingramcontent.com/pod-product-compliance
Lightning Source LLC
LaVergne TN
LVHW041300150826
845673LV00008B/2677